The Little Mermaid

A Parragon Book

Published by
Parragon Books,
Unit 13–17, Avonbridge Trading Estate,
Atlantic Road, Avonmouth, Bristol BS11 9QD

Produced by
The Templar Company plc,
Pippbrook Mill, London Road, Dorking, Surrey RH4 1JE

Designed by Mark Kingsley-Monks

Printed and bound in Italy

ISBN 0-75250-768-0

The Little Mermaid

Retold by Caroline Repchuk
Illustrated by Roger Langton

· PARRAGON ·

Once there was a little mermaid Princess, who lived with her father, the Mer King, and her five older sisters, in a beautiful coral palace beneath the sea.

She was a quiet girl, and spent most of her time alone in her garden.

Here she kept her prize possession, a marble statue of a boy which she had rescued from a shipwreck.

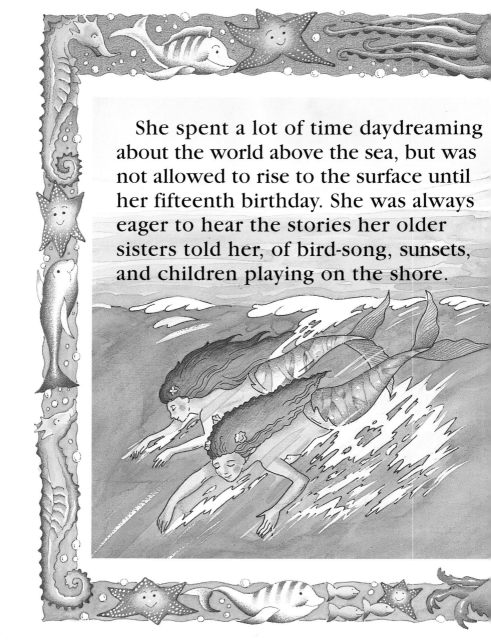

She spent a lot of time daydreaming about the world above the sea, but was not allowed to rise to the surface until her fifteenth birthday. She was always eager to hear the stories her older sisters told her, of bird-song, sunsets, and children playing on the shore.

Finally her fifteenth birthday arrived. She broke through the waves at sunset as the clouds gleamed pink and gold. It was the most beautiful sight she had ever seen. A brightly lit ship passed by, with music ringing from the decks. It was the birthday of a handsome young prince, and they were celebrating with fireworks.

But as the little mermaid gazed in wonder at the lovely sight, dark storm clouds were gathering overhead. The waves rose high and the ship was tossed up and down, before finally sinking beneath the waves.

The little mermaid was very frightened as she had never seen anything like it before, but she knew she must save the Prince. She found him clinging to a plank of wood, and, holding tight, gently carried him to shore.

She watched from the sea as a group of schoolgirls found the Prince lying motionless on the sand. Opening his eyes, the Prince saw a little girl bending over him, and mistakenly thought that it must have been she who had saved him.

Sadly, the little mermaid turned away and swam back home. She told her sisters what had happened. "If I could only see him again," she sobbed. Luckily an old merman knew where to find him and soon the six sisters had set off in search of his palace.

They arrived when the moon was high in the sky, and the marble walls of the palace gleamed in the moonlight. The little mermaid was enchanted.

After that she returned to the palace every day, to watch the Prince as he sat alone in his garden.

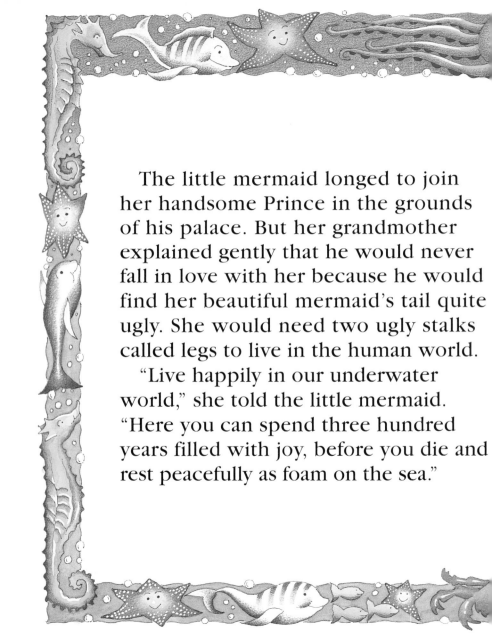

The little mermaid longed to join her handsome Prince in the grounds of his palace. But her grandmother explained gently that he would never fall in love with her because he would find her beautiful mermaid's tail quite ugly. She would need two ugly stalks called legs to live in the human world.

"Live happily in our underwater world," she told the little mermaid. "Here you can spend three hundred years filled with joy, before you die and rest peacefully as foam on the sea."

That night there was a Court Ball in the Undersea Kingdom. Hundreds of brightly coloured fish gathered to watch the mermen and mermaids dancing. The little mermaid had the sweetest voice in all the sea, and her friends all cheered as she sang for them.

But later as she sat alone in her garden the little mermaid wept bitter tears.

"If only I could join my Prince," she cried. Then in a flash, she remembered the evil sea witch. "Maybe she could help me," she murmered.

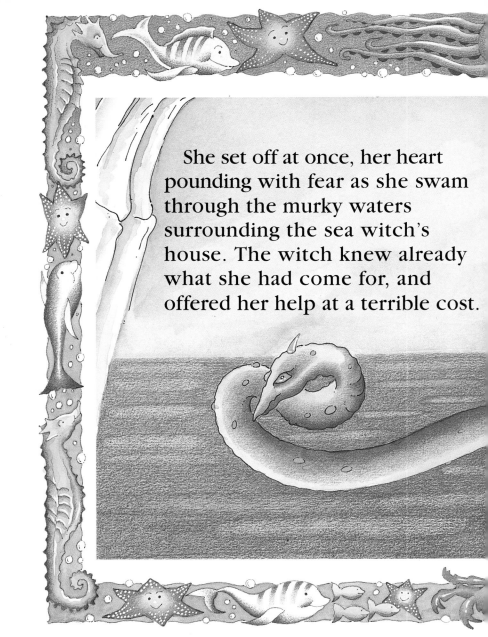

She set off at once, her heart pounding with fear as she swam through the murky waters surrounding the sea witch's house. The witch knew already what she had come for, and offered her help at a terrible cost.

The little mermaid made a deal. In return for a potion to turn her tail into legs, she gave the witch her lovely voice. The witch told her that every step she took would be like walking on knives, and she would never again be a mermaid or be able to return home.

But still the mermaid agreed and, rising through the dark waters to the world above, she waved her home goodbye forever. The Prince found her next day, lying on the palace steps. She could not speak, but he welcomed the beautiful stranger to his home, and she soon captivated his court with her sweet smile and graceful dancing.

From then on the young Prince spent all his time with her, and although every step she took was agony she never once complained. The Prince loved her dearly, but he loved her as a sister, and never once thought of marrying her.

And so in time it was arranged that
the Prince should marry a neighbouring
Princess, and he set off on the Royal
Ship to meet her. The little mermaid
was frantic with fear that she would
lose him, and he too was sad for he
wished he could find the girl who had
saved his life, and marry her instead.

Imagine the Prince's joy when the Princess turned out to be the very same girl he believed had saved him! They fell in love at once and in no time were married. The little mermaiden was heartbroken. Having failed to win the Prince's heart, she would now turn to foam on the sea, just as the sea-witch had told her.

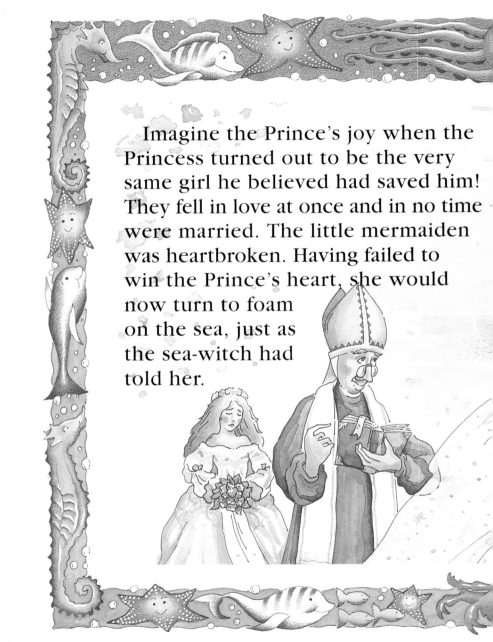

They told her they had given it to the sea-witch in exchange for a knife with which the little mermaid could kill the Prince. If she did so before sunrise, and dripped his blood on her feet, her mermaid's tail would return. Unhappily she took the knife, and went to the Prince's room.

But the little mermaid could not kill her beloved Prince for she loved him too much. So she flung the knife far out to sea and jumped overboard. But instead of dissolving into foam, she felt herself being raised up by a thousand beautiful spirits hovering in the air above her. They invited her to join them in their quest to spread health and happiness over the earth, and suddenly she felt full of joy. She smiled down at the Prince and his new bride, silently wishing them great happiness, before soaring with the spirits high into the air.

HANS CHRISTIAN ANDERSEN

Hans Christian Andersen was born
in Odense, Denmark, on April 2nd, 1805.
His family was very poor and throughout
his life he suffered much unhappiness.
Even after he had found success as a
writer, Hans Christian Andersen felt
something of an outsider, an aspect which
often emerged in his stories and can be
seen clearly here in the character of
the little Mermaid.
His fairy stories, famous throughout
the world, include *The Snow Queen*,
The Ugly Duckling and *The Emperor's
New Clothes*, and are amongst the
most frequently translated works
of literature.